D0401723

THE CASE OF THE
WEIRD BLUE
CHICKEN
the next
misadventure

Also by Doreen Cronin

Bloom
Bounce
Click, Clack, Boo!
Click, Clack, Moo: Cows That Type
Click, Clack, Peep!
Click, Clack, Quackity-Quack
Click, Clack, Splish, Splash
Dooby Dooby Moo
Duck for President
Giggle, Giggle, Quack
M.O.M. (Mom Operating Manual)
Stretch
Thump, Quack, Moo
Wiggle

The Chicken Squad #1: *The Chicken Squad*

The Chicken Squad #3: *Into the Wild*

THE CHICKEN SQUAD

THE CASE OF THE WEIRD BLUE CHICKEN

the next misadventure

Doreen Cronin

Illustrated by Kevin Cornell

A Caitlyn Dlouhy Book

Atheneum Books for Young Readers

atheneum New York London Toronto Sydney New Delhi

ATHENEUM BOOKS FOR YOUNG READERS
An imprint of Simon & Schuster Children's Publishing Division
1230 Avenue of the Americas, New York, New York 10020

Also available in an Atheneum Books for Young Readers hardcover edition.
Book design by Sonia Chaghatzbanian
The text for this book is set in Garth Graphic and Barron.
The illustrations for this book are rendered in graphite, watercolor, and digital.
Manufactured in the United States of America
1117 MTN
First Atheneum Books for Young Readers paperback edition May 2016
10 9 8 7 6
The Library of Congress has cataloged the hardcover edition as follows:
Cronin, Doreen.
The case of the weird blue chicken: the next misadventure / Doreen Cronin ; illustrated by Kevin Cornell.
p. cm. – (The Chicken Squad)
Summary: When a weird blue chicken comes to Chicken Squad headquarters for help, siblings Dirt, Sugar, Poppy, and Sweetie help find her missing house.
ISBN 978-1-4424-9679-8 (hc)
ISBN 978-1-4424-9680-4 (pbk)
ISBN 978-1-4424-9681-1 (eBook)
[1. Chickens–Fiction. 2. Blue jay–Fiction. 3. Lost and found possessions–Fiction. 4. Humorous stories. 5. Mystery and detective stories.] I. Cornell, Kevin, illustrator. II. Title. III. Title: The case of the weird blue chicken.
PZ7.C88135Cas 2014
[E]–dc23 2013032099

To Kevin Cornell

—D. C.

Doreen! I'm so *flattered*!

—K. C.

Chapter 1

Dirt.

Sugar.
Poppy.
Sweetie.

You lost it.
We'll find it.

You broke it?
We'll fix it.

In trouble?
We'll get you out.

Looking for trouble?
We'll bring it to you.

Chapter 2

I found the Chicken Squad flyer underneath my dog bowl this morning. I have been sharing a backyard with those four featherballs for two years. I already had all the information I needed about them, but you might not. Here's what you need to know:

Dirt: Short, yellow, fuzzy

Real Name: Peep

Specialty: Foreign languages, math, colors, computer codes

Sugar: Short, yellow, fuzzy

Real Name: Little Boo

Specialty: Breaking and entering, interrupting

Poppy: Short, yellow, fuzzy

Real Name: Poppy

Specialty: Watching the shoe (will explain later)

Sweetie: Short, yellow, fuzzy

Real Name: Sweet Coconut Louise

Specialty: None that I can see

They know trouble all right. They know how to *cause* it. Can they get you out of it? Not a chance. Will they make a heap of it if you leave them alone for more than two and a half minutes? You bet they will. And not the easy kind of trouble, either, like

"Oops, I have a paper clip stuck in my nostril." The hard kind of trouble. The ransom-note, accidental-fire, wing-in-a-sling, my-brother-is-stuck-in-the-garden-hose kind of trouble. And they manage to make that kind of trouble almost every single day.

Despite all the commotion, all the squawking, and a handful of life-or-death situations, things seem to work out. There's one reason for that. It's not Dirt, Sugar, Poppy, or Sweetie, and it's not even their eagle-eyed mother, Moosh. It's me. J. J. Tully. Retired search-and-rescue dog, seven years on the job, two years in the yard.

My advice? Keep an eye on them at all times.

Chapter 3

"Can I help you?" asked Sugar.

It was early Tuesday morning. A tiny blue bird had just shown up in the chicken coop. The ground was still wet from the sprinkler. She didn't wipe her feet before she came in.

"I have a problem," said the little bird.

"You sure do," answered Sugar. "You are leaving footprints all over my floor."

"Oh, sorry," answered the little bird.

"Uh-huh," said Sugar. Sugar came out from behind the old shoe she was using for a desk. "How did you find us?"

"The giant sign outside the chicken coop," answered the bird. "Plus, there are these flyers all over the place." She handed Sugar a stack of fifteen flyers.

"Did anybody follow you here?" asked Dirt.

"I don't think so," said the little bird.

"Check the door," said Sugar.

The little bird went toward the door.

"Not you, little bird," said Sugar, looking directly at her sister Dirt.

Dirt jumped up out of the old shoe. She walked to the door.

"Any more chicks in that desk?" asked the little bird, pointing at the shoe.

"I'll ask the questions," answered Sugar.

Sugar made some observations:

Small
Blue
Tiny feet
Wings
Possibly a weird blue chicken

"Do you lay eggs?" asked Sugar.

"That's a very strange question," said the little bird.

Sugar made a new observation:

Weird blue chicken does
not like to answer questions.

"I just need one more thing," said Sugar. She pulled a cotton swab out of the shoe.

"What's that for?" asked the little bird.

"I'm going to scrape under your arm with it."

"Why would you do that?" asked the little bird.

"For the smell," answered Sugar. "I give it to my dog friend, J. J. Now, hold still . . ."

"I do not want my armpit scraped with a cotton swab," said the little bird. She backed away toward the door.

"Fine by me, Weird Blue Chicken,"

said Sugar. "But if we can't smell you, we probably can't find you."

"I'm right here," said the little bird.

"You can go now," said Sugar. "I've got your number. If you ever get lost, the Chicken Squad *might* be able to find you. It will be tough without your smell on file, but we'll try. Don't say I didn't warn you. Have a nice day."

The little bird did not move.

"Go on, scram," said Sugar. "Get out of here." Sugar went back behind the desk and picked up a tiny piece of newspaper she'd found on the ground.

Again, the little bird did not move.

Sugar put down the newspaper bit. "Are you lost?"

"No."

"Did you *lose* something?" asked Sugar.

"No."

Sweetie stuck her head out of the shoe.

"How many chickens are in that thing?" asked the little bird.

"For someone who walked in off the

street, you sure do ask a lot of questions," said Sugar. She came out from behind the desk and stood next to Dirt. "I'm gonna keep my eye on you, Weird Blue Chicken."

"Hang on, Sugar," said Dirt. "I've got one more question before she goes."

"What's that?" asked Sugar.

"Do you need help, little bird?" asked Dirt.

"Yes," answered the little bird.

"Then you've come to the right place," said Dirt, wrapping her wing around the little bird. "What seems to be the problem?" Up close, Dirt could see that the little blue bird had tiny blue bird eyes. And there were tears in them.

Chapter 4

The little blue bird took a deep breath. "I have a really big problem."

Dirt and Sugar exchanged glances.

"What is it, Weird Blue Chicken?" asked Sugar. "What seems to be your problem?"

"It's a bird," answered the little bird.

"What does he look like?" asked Dirt.

"He's six feet tall," answered the bird.

"Are you sure about that?" asked Sugar.

"Yes, I'm sure," answered the bird.

"Birds don't come in that size," said Sugar. "You must have had a bad dream. I can't help you if your problem is a big bird bad dream."

Dirt looked Weird Blue Chicken up and down.

"How tall are you?" she asked.

"I'm about four feet tall," answered the little bird.

"Ah, I see," said Dirt kindly. "I think you are confusing inches with feet. It's a common mistake. You are about four *inches* tall."

The little bird shrugged.

Sugar rolled her eyes.

"What else can you tell me about this bird?" asked Dirt.

"He's yellow," answered the bird.

"Can you be more specific, ma'am?" asked Dirt. "For example, I'm kind of a

canary yellow. Sugar is kind of a dandelion yellow. Let me get my crayon box . . ."

"Pipe down," said Sugar. "Let the chicken talk."

The little bird said nothing.

"Back to this other bird," said Sugar. Her voice was serious. "You said he was in some kind of trouble."

"No," said the little bird. "He *is* the trouble."

"That's odd," said Sugar. "Birds don't usually cause trouble."

"Actually, birds cause trouble all the time," said Dirt.

"Pipe down!" said Sugar. "Let the chicken talk."

The little bird still said nothing.

"What exactly do you think this bird did?" asked Dirt, using her kindest voice.

"He kidnapped my house."

"That is a very serious accusation, Weird Blue Chicken!" said Sugar. "What kind of proof do you have?"

"He's sitting in my house, and he won't leave," answered the little bird.

"House-kidnapping is kind of an awkward phrase," said Dirt. "I think we should call it a house-napping."

"Pipe down!" said Sugar. "Let the chicken talk."

The little bird said nothing.

"What makes you so sure it's a bird?" asked Sugar.

"I know a bird when I see one," said the little bird.

"You don't know an *inch* when you

see one," said Sugar. "How can I be sure that you know what a bird looks like?"

"How do you know he won't leave?" asked Dirt.

"I asked him to leave," said the little bird. "And he said no."

"Interesting," said Sugar. She went to the door and tucked her wings behind her back. She was deep in thought. After seventy-three seconds of silence, she made an observation in her notebook:

Have been standing here a long time. Should turn around.

She turned to face the little bird. "I know what you need," declared Sugar.

"I need that bird out of my house," said the little bird.

"No," said Sugar. "You need the Chicken Squad."

"Can the Chicken Squad get that bird out of my house?" asked the little bird.

"I have absolutely no idea, ma'am," answered Dirt. "No idea at all."

"Today is your lucky day," announced Sugar. "The Chicken Squad will take your case. It will be dangerous. It will be hard, and it will require your full cooperation. Do you understand?"

"Yes," said the little bird.

"Good," said Sugar. "Now, please go." She leaned in close to the little bird and whispered, "Stay low. Keep

your head down. Walk only in the shadows. Don't attract any attention. Don't tell anyone we spoke. And tweet three times when the coast is clear."

"I usually just fly away," said the little bird.

"That's fine, too," said Sugar.

Chapter 5

"We forgot to ask her where she lives," said Dirt. Sugar was pacing back and forth in the coop.

"We're going to follow her," said Sugar.

"Why didn't we just go with her?" asked Dirt.

"I don't trust her," said Sugar.

"Why not?" asked Dirt.

"Never trust a weird blue chicken," said Sugar. She shook her head. "You've got a lot to learn, little sis. It's a tough world out there. Nothing is as it seems."

"I'm pretty sure she's a blue jay," said Dirt, "not a weird blue chicken."

"Pipe down," said Sugar. "Let the chicken talk."

"Um . . . she's not here anymore," said Dirt.

"Right," said Sugar. "C'mon, let's go. I don't want to lose her trail."

"What should I do?" asked Sweetie.

"Stay in the shoe," said Sugar. "In case another client comes in."

"Got it," said Sweetie.

A moment later she asked, "What should I do if another client *does* come in?"

"Tell them to make an appointment," said Sugar. "Then get back in the shoe."

"Got it," said Sweetie.

Sugar and Dirt walked side by side. They made a left turn, staying close to the shadows. Then they made another left turn. They walked single file against the back wall. They made another left turn.

"Now what?" asked Dirt.

"Turn left," said Sugar.

They turned left.

"We are right back where we started," said Dirt.

"Exactly," said Sugar. "Look behind you."

Dirt looked over her shoulder.

"I don't see anything," said Dirt.

"Exactly," said Sugar. "Now we know we're not being followed."

"Wow," said Dirt. "That was really smart."

"Stick with me, kid," said Sugar. "I know how the world works."

"Can I come with you guys?" Dirt

and Sugar turned around to find the little blue bird right behind them.

"Weird Blue Chicken! Where did you come from?" asked Sugar.

"I followed you," said the little bird.

"How?" asked Sugar.

"I stayed low. Kept my head down. Walked only in the shadows. And didn't attract any attention."

A slow smile spread across Sugar's face. "You're a fast learner."

"But *why* did you follow us?" asked Dirt.

"Because I don't

trust you," said the little bird. "Never trust a small, yellow bird with glasses. You've got a lot to learn, kid."

"I like the way you think, Weird Blue Chicken," said Sugar.

Chapter 6

Sugar, Dirt, and the little blue bird tiptoed across the yard. They stopped in the middle of the lawn and waited for the sprinkler to switch to the other side.

"It's right back here," said the little bird. "It's the oak tree. I call her Duncan."

"You named your tree?" asked Sugar.

"Of course," said the little bird. "Never trust a bird who doesn't name her tree."

"Of course," said Dirt.

"I told you she was weird," whispered Sugar.

The oak tree was the tallest tree in the yard. With the thick leaves of summer, it looked like a solid wall of green. It was impossible to see anything hidden behind it.

"Where's your nest?" asked Dirt.

"I don't have a nest," said the little bird. "I have a house."

"That's a little strange, don't you think?" asked Sugar. "Birds are supposed to build nests, not live in houses."

"Do you live in a nest?" asked the little blue bird.

"Of course not," said Sugar. "I'm a chicken. I live in a chicken coop."

"And I'm a bird," said the little bird. "So I live in a birdhouse."

"You've got me there, Weird Blue Chicken," said Sugar.

"I don't see it," said Dirt. "I don't see your house."

The little bird hopped from place to place on the ground below the tree. "It should be right up there," she said. "This is where it's always been—about seven inches off the ground. It's red. It has a hole in the middle for a door, and a beautiful slanted green roof. It's about eight feet high and four feet wide." Dirt pulled out a sketchpad and a box of crayons from behind her back.

"Somebody get this kid a ruler," said Sugar.

"It's okay," said Dirt. "I know she means eight *inches* high and four *inches* wide, and it's about seven *feet* off the ground."

Sugar walked around the base of the tree. "I don't see it, ma'am," she said. "I'm starting to think you dragged us all out here for nothing,"

Dirt turned her sketchpad around. "Is this it?"

"That's it!" The little bird gasped. "How did you do that?"

"I'm a good listener," said Dirt. "Red house, square front, round hole, green slanted roof."

"Wait just one minute," said Sugar.

"Describe this house-napper again. This time I want details."

"Well, he's short, yellow, and kind of fuzzy," said the little bird.

"Hmm," said Sugar. "Anything else? A tattoo? A limp? A dangerous-looking scar?"

"I don't remember any scars or tattoos," said the little bird.

Dirt showed her a sketch.

"Not quite," said the little bird. "His head is weird. It looks like an egg."

Dirt adjusted the sketch.

"Not quite," said the little bird. "His eyes are more round." Dirt adjusted the sketch again.

"Closer," said the little bird. "He's got two orange feathers sticking out of the top of his lumpy head. They are about two feet long."

"Inches, kid, INCHES!" snapped Sugar.

Dirt adjusted the sketch AGAIN.

"That's him!" screamed the little bird. "You did it! That's the egg-headed bird who stole my house."

"Oh, brother," said Dirt. She passed the sketch to Sugar.

"Oh, brother," said Sugar.

"That is no egg-headed little bird," said Dirt.

"It isn't?" asked the little bird.

"That, madam," said Dirt and Sugar, "is our brother!"

"Oh, brother," said the little bird.

"You can say that again," said Sugar.

"Oh, brother," said the little bird.

"Knock that off, kid," said Sugar.

Chapter 7

"We've got to find your brother," said the little bird.

"We've got to find your house first," said Sugar. "Poppy will be inside the house."

"What's a poppy?" asked the little bird.

"Our brother. His name is Poppy," answered Sugar.

"Where would he take a birdhouse?" asked Dirt.

"Don't you mean *why* would he take a birdhouse?" asked the little bird.

Dirt and Sugar looked at each other.

"He's kind of . . . unpredictable," said Sugar.

Dirt nodded in agreement.

"Did you have anything valuable in the house?" asked Sugar.

"Absolutely not. Not at all. Nope. Nothing. Why would I have anything valuable? That's ridiculous. Where would I even get anything valuable? I mean, really. I'm just a bird. Boring blue jay, actually. What a strange question. Now that I think about it, I believe that the contents of my house are none of your business! Good day, sir!"

Sugar made an observation.

Weird blue chicken is lying.

Dirt and Sugar watched the little bird fly away.

"Weird Blue Chicken is lying," said Sugar.

"Should we follow her?" asked Dirt.

"Nope," answered Sugar. "She's scared. She'll be back."

"We should go," said Dirt. "Right now."

"What's your hurry?" said Sugar.

"The sprinkler is—"

Dirt pulled out a pink, polka-dotted umbrella from behind her back. She held it over their heads as the water came down.

"—coming back," said Dirt.

"How do you do that?" asked Sugar.

"No idea," said Dirt.

"Impressive," said Sugar.

Chapter 8

"We have to find the little blue bird," said Dirt. She was pacing back and forth in the chicken coop.

"We don't have her scent," said Sugar. "She refused the Q-tips. At least now we know why."

"Why?" asked Dirt.

"The same reason anyone refuses

the Q-tips," said Sugar. "She has something to hide."

"We need J. J. on this," said Dirt.

"I just told you we don't have her scent. J. J. won't be able to find her without it," said Sugar.

"I might be able to help," said Sweetie.

"You helped us already, Sweetie,"

said Dirt. "You did a great job watching the shoe."

"No, really," said Sweetie. "I think I can help."

"That would be great, Sweetie," said Sugar. She patted her sister on the head. "Now, why don't you go back in the shoe and keep an eye out?"

"But . . . ," said Sweetie.

"Back in the shoe, please," said Sugar. "We need you there."

Sweetie shrugged and hopped into the shoe.

"I knew that weird blue chicken was bad news," said Sugar. "Maybe we can set a trap for her. . . ."

"What kind of trap?" asked Dirt.

"I'm not sure," said Sugar. "Let me think about it."

"I'll tell you what I think," said Sweetie from inside the shoe. "I think you better go find Grumpy Squirrel."

"Why in the world would you think that?" asked Sugar.

Sweetie stuck her hand out of the shoe. She held a note:

Dear Chicken Squad,
Someone has been stealing my acorns.
I'd like to borrow a hammer.
Signed,
Grumpy Squirrel

DEAR
CHICKEN SQUAD,
SOMEONE HAS BEEN
STEALING MY ACORNS.
I'D LIKE TO
BORROW A
HAMMER.
SIGNED, Grumpy Squirrel

"We've got a crime spree on our hands!" cried Sugar. "First a stolen birdhouse, and now Grumpy Squirrel's acorns! Something tells me they're connected. Let's go talk to Grumpy Squirrel."

"Nice work, Sweetie," said Dirt.

"I knew the shoe was the right place for you," said Sugar.

Chapter 9

"Which tree is the Grumpy Squirrel tree?" asked Dirt.

"We'll find it," said Sugar. "Give me that note."

Sugar closed her eyes and sniffed the note.

"As I suspected," she announced. "It smells like squirrel."

"Now what?" asked Dirt.

"Now we follow the trail," said Sugar.

Sugar, Dirt, and Sweetie made four left turns around the chicken coop to make sure they weren't being followed. Sugar stopped every few feet and sniffed. She was hot on the squirrel's trail. Her eyes were squinty. Her face was serious. Her head was down.

Sugar walked across the yard, hopped over the sprinkler, and then circled the bottom of a giant maple tree.

"This is it," she said. "The trail ends

here. This must be where Grumpy Squirrel lives."

Dirt and Sugar looked up. Grumpy Squirrel was looking down at them.

"Wow," said Dirt. "You did it! You tracked Grumpy Squirrel!"

"Of course I did," asked Sugar. "The wet earth from the sprinkler really helps to raise the scent."

"There's also this obvious trail of

squirrel footprints in the mud," said Sweetie.

"I thought we left you in the shoe," said Sugar.

"How are we going to get up there?" asked Dirt.

"We're not," said Sugar. "He'll come down."

The three chicks waited at the base of the tree.

"Fancy meeting you here!" Grumpy Squirrel yelled down.

"We got your note," said Dirt.

"Did you bring the hammer?" asked Grumpy Squirrel.

Sweetie held a hammer up for Grumpy Squirrel to see.

"Good work," said Grumpy Squirrel. He climbed down the trunk of the tree and took the hammer from Sweetie.

"Whoa!" said Sugar. She grabbed the hammer back. "Wait just a second there, Grumpy Squirrel. First, you're going to tell me exactly what kind of

plans you have that require a hammer. It's a little odd for a tree rodent to need one, don't you think?"

"I'm just going to crack open some acorns," answered Grumpy Squirrel.

"But I thought all your acorns had been stolen," said Dirt.

"I have some . . . emergency acorns," answered Grumpy Squirrel. "But they are old and a little stale. I, um, need the hammer to get them open."

Grumpy Squirrel grabbed the hammer from Sugar and darted up the tree. Dirt jumped on his tail. Sugar jumped on Dirt. Sweetie jumped on Sugar.

"Hang on!" yelled Dirt.

Grumpy Squirrel ran full speed up the trunk of the tree and then made a sharp left turn. He ran to the end of a branch and then leaped off it, flying through the air and aiming for a branch of the neighboring tree.

He missed.

"AAAAAHHHH!" yelled Grumpy Squirrel.

"AAAAAAAAAAAAAHHHH-HHH!!" yelled Sugar.

"AAAAAAAAAAAAAAAAAHHH-HHHHHHHHHHH!!" yelled Dirt.

"AAAAAAAAAAAAAAAAAAAAAA-AAAAAAAAAAAAAAAAHHHHHHH-HHHHHHHHHHHHHHHHHHHHH-HHHHHHHHHH!!" yelled Sweetie.

Chapter 10

Dirt, Sugar, Sweetie, and Grumpy Squirrel hung like a vine, swaying back and forth, back and forth.

"HELP!" screamed Sweetie. She held on tight to Sugar's scrawny chicken foot as Sugar held on tight to Dirt's scrawny chicken foot, and Dirt held on tight to the pink, polka-dotted umbrella that had hooked onto Grumpy Squirrel's hammer, which was stuck on something in the leaves.

"You're only nine feet off the ground! Stop screaming and just let go!" yelled the little blue bird as she ran out of the bushes nearby.

"Nine feet!" yelled Sweetie. **"HELP!"**

"She means *inches*!" yelled Dirt.

"You're only nine *inches* off the ground. Just let go of Sugar before you pull us all down!"

"HEEEELLLLLPP!" screamed Sweetie.

The branch bobbed up and down from the extra weight of three chickens, an umbrella, a squirrel, and a hammer.

Up and down. Up and down. Up and down.

Up and—

Crack.

Thud. Thud. Thud. Thud. Thud.

Wait for it.

THUD.

Chapter 11

"Look out below!" came a voice from above.

Sugar, Dirt, Sweetie, and Grumpy Squirrel looked up just in time to see a little red house with a green slanted roof falling from the tree. Sticking out of the hole in the middle were two funky orange feathers, attached to the

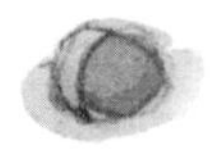

lumpy, egg head of their brother.

"Poppy!!" yelled Dirt and Sugar.

THUD!!

The house landed with a crash, and split open. Dozens and dozens of acorns scattered across the ground.

"I guess I won't need the hammer anymore," said Grumpy Squirrel. He scurried along the ground, picking up as many acorns as he could.

Sugar, Dirt, and Sweetie rushed over to their brother and helped him get up onto his feet.

"Are you okay?" asked Sweetie.

"I'm fine," answered Poppy. "I'm just glad to be out of that tree!"

"What were you doing up there?" asked Sugar.

"It smells better than the shoe," said Poppy.

"Can't argue with that," said Sweetie.

"I got stuck," answered Poppy. "That hole in the front was not built for a well-fed chicken. Grumpy Squirrel found me, and then he moved the whole house!"

"Look what you've done to my bird-house!" cried the little blue bird.

"Tough break, Weird Blue Chicken," said Sugar. "But that's the price you pay for stealing acorns."

"I am not a Weird Blue Chicken!"

said the little blue bird. "Why can't you just call me by my real name?"

"Simple," said Sugar. "You never told me your name."

"My name is Winnie," she said. "I'm a blue jay."

"Not from around here, are you, Winnie?" asked Sugar.

"How did you know?" asked Winnie.

"We have rules in the yard," said Sugar. "Acorns belong to the finder."

"Well, it's not fair!" cried Winnie. "Grumpy Squirrel hogs *all* the acorns! They are supposed to be for everybody!"

"She has a point, Grumpy Squirrel,"

said Dirt. "Seems like there should be enough acorns to go around."

"I need *all* the acorns," explained Grumpy Squirrel. "They're the only things I eat."

"That might explain why you are so grumpy," said Sugar.

"Here," said Dirt. She held out a strawberry. "Try this."

Grumpy Squirrel sniffed the fruit for a second and then took a teeny, tiny bite.

"Not bad," he said. "Not bad at all."

"Okay, picnic's over," said Sugar. "Grumpy Squirrel needs to try new foods, and Winnie here needs to follow the rules. Everybody clear?"

"I'm sorry about the acorns," said Winnie.

"It's okay, kid," said Sugar. "Just don't do it again."

"I won't. I promise," said Winnie.

"One more thing, kid," said Sugar.

"What is it?" asked Winnie.

"See that big house over there? Well, there's a lady in the house. Her name is Barbara. She feeds us, she feeds the dog, and she'll feed you, too. That funny-looking thing hanging by the back door is a bird feeder. All you can eat. No charge."

"Thanks, Sugar," said Winnie.

"Anytime, kid," said Sugar. "Now, stay out of trouble."

Winnie started to hop away.

"One more thing, kid," said Sugar.

"Yes?"

"You owe me a cotton-swabbed armpit," said Sugar.

"I still think that's weird," said Winnie.

"The world is weird, kid," said Sugar. "Get used to it."

Epilogue

So there you have it. The Chicken Squad saves the day. Sugar was right all along. Never trust a weird blue chicken. Plus eat some fruit. Those are just my observations. You're welcome. You can make your own.

Turn the page for a sneak peek at
The Chicken Squad #3:

Yet another misadventure

"I got a bad feeling about that new box over there," said Sugar. She pointed to a strange wooden structure on the other side of the yard. It stood on tall legs a few feet off the ground.

"Why?" asked Dirt.

"Why would Barbara sneak a weird box into our yard under the cover of night? What doesn't she want us to know? What is she hiding?"

"Actually," said Dirt, "Barbara's been out there hammering and sawing and building every single afternoon for the last two weeks."

"I think I would have noticed that, Dirt," said Sugar. She hopped up onto

the picnic bench. "I'm very observant."

"She also dismantled our chicken coop yesterday and moved it to the other side of the yard."

"I think I would have noticed that, Dirt," said Sugar.

"You may have been napping," suggested Dirt.

"What I hear you saying," said Sugar, "is that Barbara built a top-secret box and then top secretly moved our chicken coop far, far away from it. That's what I hear you saying. . . . "

"I didn't say that . . . ," said Dirt.

"Fine," answered Sugar, "but that's what I heard."

"Okay, well, why don't we just go take a closer look? There's a ramp that leads right up to the front of the box," suggested Dirt. "Maybe we can get some more information."

"We have no idea what kind of wild creature is in there!" said Sugar. "All we know for sure is that whatever it is, it is very, very dangerous."

"How do we know that?" asked Dirt.

"If it wasn't wild and dangerous, why would Barb keep it in a box? Only wild, dangerous animals are KEPT IN BOXES!"

"But we live in a box," said Dirt, "and we're not dangerous."

"Speak for yourself," replied Sugar.

"Anyway," said Dirt, "I think what we need to do here is observe and investigate."

"What I hear you saying," said Sugar, "is that this is an extremely dangerous

situation, lives are at stake, and we should proceed with caution. That's what I hear you saying. . . ."

"I didn't say that," said Dirt. "I didn't say that at all."

"Fine," said Sugar. "But that's what I heard."

The Guardians

by WILLIAM JOYCE

An epic battle of good versus evil—
starring your worst nightmares and
your all-time favorite heroes.

The books that inspired
**The Rise
of the
Guardians**
movie.

"*Nicholas St. North and the Battle of the Nightmare King* stole my son! The book came into our house, and the boy disappeared, for hours. Eventually he returned, but it seems that his imagination never came all the way back. A part of him will always remain tangled in the deep, dark, dazzling, insouciant mythology of this latest and most wonderful of William Joyce's worlds."
—Michael Chabon, winner of the Pulitzer Prize

A Caitlyn Dlouhy Book • A Moonbot Book
SimonandSchuster.com/KIDS • PRINT AND EBOOK EDITIONS AVAILABLE

Meet a little girl
with a lot
of big ideas!
VIOLET MACKEREL'S
brilliant plot
Anna Branford
illustrated by
Elanna Allen
VIOLET MACKEREL'S
remarkable recovery
Anna Branford
illustrated by
Elanna Allen
VIOLET MACKEREL'S
natural habitat
Anna Branford
illustrated by
Elanna Allen
VIOLET MACKEREL'S
personal space
Anna Branford
illustrated by
Elanna Allen
VIOLET MACKEREL'S
possible friend
Anna Branford
illustrated by
Elanna Allen
VIOLET MACKEREL'S
pocket protest
Anna Branford
illustrated by
Elanna Allen
atheneum
KIDS.SimonandSchuster.com
PRINT AND EBOOK EDITIONS AVAILABLE